KIDS CAN'T STOP READING THE CHOOSE YOUR OWN ADVENTURE® STORIES!

"Choose Your Own Adventure is the best thing that has come along since books themselves."
—Alysha Beyer, age 11

"I didn't read much before, but now I read my Choose Your Own Adventure books almost every night."
—Chris Brogan, age 13

"I love the control I have over what happens next."
—Kosta Efstathiou, age 17

"Choose Your Own Adventure books are so much fun to read and collect—I want them all!"
—Brendan Davin, age 11

And teachers like this series, too:
"We have read and reread, worn thin, loved, loaned, bought for others, and donated to school libraries our Choose Your Own Adventure books."

CHOOSE YOUR OWN ADVENTURE®— AND MAKE READING MORE FUN!

PLANET OF THE DRAGONS

BY RICHARD BRIGHTFIELD

ILLUSTRATED BY JUDITH MITCHELL

An Edward Packard Book

BANTAM BOOKS
TORONTO • NEW YORK • LONDON • SYDNEY • AUCKLAND

RL 4, IL age 10 and up

PLANET OF THE DRAGONS
A Bantam Book / January 1988
3 printings through April 1988

CHOOSE YOUR OWN ADVENTURE® *is a registered trademark
of Bantam Books, a division of Bantam Doubleday Dell
Publishing Group, Inc. Registered in U.S. Patent and
Trademark Office and elsewhere.*

Original conception of Edward Packard.

*Cover art by James Warhola
Inside Illustrations by Judith Mitchell*

ISBN 0-553-26887-2

Published simultaneously in the United States and Canada

Bantam Books are published by Bantam Books, a division of
Bantam Doubleday Dell Publishing Group, Inc. Its trademark,
consisting of the words "Bantam Books" and the portrayal of a
rooster, is Registered in U.S. Patent and Trademark Office and
in other countries. Marca Registrada. Bantam Books, 666 Fifth
Avenue, New York, New York 10103.

PRINTED IN THE UNITED STATES OF AMERICA

O   12 11 10 9 8 7 6

WARNING!!!

Do not read this book straight through from beginning to end. You will have many different adventures when you land on a distant planet that's inhabited by fire-breathing dragons.

As you read along, you will be able to make choices. Your choices will determine what happens to you next. Will you defeat the dragons before they defeat you?

Think carefully before you make a choice. The fearsome dragons aren't the only strange creatures on the planet of Tambor.

Good luck!

You stare forlornly at your cramped surroundings—the curved titanium shell that encloses you and its tightly packed array of instrumentation. Will you ever get out of this life pod? you wonder. According to the computer, your life pod is now approaching a planet. It looks a lot like Earth from outer space. But you know it isn't Earth. Your home planet is hundreds of light years away.

While on a scouting mission in the Cetus quadrant, you were captured by the Taurons, an evil race that carved out an empire among the stars. The Taurons took you to their home planet and forced you into service as a cadet in their space corps. Then, during a fight with their major enemy, the Vorks, your spaceship was destroyed. You alone escaped—barely—in this small life pod.

Suddenly the pod skims over rough terrain. As it touches down the pod bounces across the ground, then crashes into the side of a huge boulder.

Turn to page 6.

"There's plenty of water down there," Millie's father says, as your ship cruises 80,000 kilometers above Alcor's fifth planet. "We've orbited three times, and now I know why this planet is listed as unsafe for landing. It's completely covered with water! There's no place to land at all—and this ship won't float. It would sink like a rock."

"What are we going to do?" Millie asks.

"We may as well go down to the surface and make sure there's no place to land," you say. "Maybe there's a shallow place somewhere."

Millie and her father agree. There's no other choice at this point. You've already used up too much fuel to make it to Earth without refueling.

Cautiously you descend through the vaporous atmosphere of the water planet. For thousands of kilometers you skim along the surface. You're using a tremendous amount of fuel to overcome atmospheric drag, but it doesn't matter now. You're past the point of no return.

Suddenly Millie screams. "I see something over there—an island!"

Turn to page 90.

"This is an acoustic bottle," the professor says. "The note made by this end of the bottle attracts the dragons, while the other note drives them away. This and other experiments have led me to believe that the space dragons are not true life forms at all but are machines—mechanical monsters that arrived here accidentally from another planetary system."

"Living here on Tambor, we know all about real dragons," Keesa says. "Once, native dragons roamed the planet, but they always lived peacefully with other creatures. Now the few that are left hide in caves, for they are more terrified of the space dragons than any other creature on our planet."

"But why are the space dragons destroying your planet?" you ask.

"I've given a lot of thought to that also," says Dr. Nekai. "I think they're a kind of weapon. Perhaps they were sent to fight a different enemy, but they went astray and accidentally found this planet. Tambor probably resembles the target planet in some basic way."

"Maybe we could drive them off Tambor with your acoustic bottle," Keesa says.

Turn to page 12.

"How . . . how do you know my language?" you ask.

"It's *you* who knows your language, not me," the creature replies.

"You mean you can read my mind?" you ask.

"Not your *mind*, as you call it, but the language in your head. There were once so many different languages here that people were forced to develop this power so they could communicate. I knew right away that yours is an off-world tongue. My name, by the way, is Keesa, and I am a Dern, one of the tribes of the planet, Tambor. Our planet used to be a beautiful place, with unblemished forests and lakes and fine cities—but that was before the space dragons came and began destroying everything."

"Dragons—from space?" you ask in astonishment.

Turn to page 17.

Keesa climbs out of the hole. You're right behind him, and luckily there's no sign of the space dragons!

"I'm going back to search in the library in Shanar," Keesa says as he sets off at a brisk pace. "I must try to find a way to defeat the dragons. You may come with me if you wish, but it would be safer for you to stay underground. I can show you a tunnel entrance near here—the tunnel leads to the realm of the Derns, far beneath the ground. My people there will help you."

*If you go with Keesa to Shanar,
turn to page 24.*

*If you decide to go underground,
turn to page 70.*

Shaken, but unharmed, you stagger out through the hatch. Your legs feel as stiff as an old dog's. From a quick examination of the life pod, you can tell that it will never fly again. Its nose is crumpled, its fins are broken off, and its electronic and power systems are knocked out. At least your

emergency food supplies are intact, and your chemical analyzer is working. The atmosphere of the planet is thin, but you're able to breathe, so when your legs regain their strength, the going should be fairly easy.

Turn to page 105.

You and Keesa hike along the bottom of the cliff.

Suddenly, a huge form emerges from the mists at the base of the cliff. It looks like a giant caterpillar, bristling with immensely long hairs. Another of the enormous creatures emerges behind it.

"Don't be alarmed," Keesa says, sensing your fright. "The Nedigs won't attack us. They are just curious."

"I hope they're not *too* curious," you say. "I'd hate to have one crawl over me—each one must weigh a hundred tons."

"They are usually friendly," Keesa says. "In fact, that gives me an idea."

Keesa gives a high-pitched whistle. A few seconds later one of the Nedigs makes a similar sound.

"When the Nedig gets close enough, grab hold of its hair and hang on," Keesa says.

"Grab hold? But what—" you start to ask.

"Quick!" Keesa exclaims. "Here it comes now!"

Turn to page 26.

Before you leave for the Darblon Mountains, Dr. Nekai hands you one of his acoustic bottles. "This may protect you," he says. "While you're gone, I will build an even stronger one." He shows you and Keesa to a stairway that leads back up to the surface. There he wishes you good luck and bids you farewell.

You and Keesa set out at a fast pace over the plain. From time to time you cast your eyes around the sky. Thankfully, you see no sign of the dragons. Soon you come to a broad riverbed. It's certain that once a great river flowed here, but now there's only the barest trickle of water.

"This dry riverbed shall serve as our road," says Keesa. "It will take us to the Great Rift, which lies between us and the Darblon Mountains."

"Great Rift?" you repeat. "What's that?"

"It's hard to describe," Keesa replies. "You'll just have to see it when we get there."

Turn to page 45.

"Those are tympors!" Keesa exclaims. "I wonder what they are doing in the city. I thought they were almost extinct. My people used to tame them and ride them. Before the space dragons came, there were large herds of tympors wandering across the plains; now they are very rare."

You look over the wall. Several tall, four-footed animals are grazing nearby. They resemble horses, except their legs are longer and very thin. Their heads are also long and thin, with round, oversized ears at one end and two sets of eyes on stalks at the other.

"They must be scavenging for food," Keesa says. "There were once huge storehouses of grain in the city. Most were burned by the dragons."

Suddenly, the tympors turn away from you and strain their ears as if they're listening for something. Their eyes wobble at the ends of their stalks. Keesa, who is facing in the same direction, also becomes rigid.

"The dragons are coming back! We'll either have to get out of the city fast or hide underground. I can't take responsibility for your life; the choice must be yours."

*If you set out across the countryside,
turn to page 84.*

If you hide underground, turn to page 20.

"I have not yet been able to make a strong enough bottle," Dr. Nekai says. "The sounds have a limited range. There's no way I could cover the whole planet. But there is this to think about: Since the dragons are only machines, they must also have a base where they are serviced and repaired, probably by robots that come with them. According to my calculations, that base shouldn't be far from here. If someone could sabotage it so the dragons couldn't be maintained, they would eventually break down—every one of them. And we'd be rid of them."

Turn to page 16.

In a moment all is quiet again. The dots have disappeared and the structure is now hidden by a pall of smoke. You return to the wreckage of the pod and try to get the emergency rescue signal working, but the power cells have all been destroyed. You remove your food and water rations, all-weather parka, chemical analyzer, lightweight tent, utility knife, flashlight, and first-aid kit. Then carefully you load them into your backpack. You decide to leave behind your other supplies— ropes, cameras, and heavy tools. You may have to travel a long way before you can find food, water, and shelter.

Again you look around at the strange landscape as you try to determine which way to go. The geometric structure you saw is still obscured by smoke. You'd like to find civilization, but you don't want to walk into a battleground. Maybe you should head for the hills.

If you go toward the hills, turn to page 32.

If you head across the plains toward the smoke, turn to page 19.

Standing there in front of you is a small figure with a beard that stretches all the way to the ground. He is clearly a Dern, like Keesa, though certainly a strange-looking one. The figure beckons for both of you to follow him into a brightly lit space off the crumbling tunnel. You find yourself in a room lined with shelves of glass and ceramic jars of every possible shape and size. A crystalline sphere caps each jar.

Keesa and the bearded Dern talk excitedly to each other in a strange language.

"I am Dr. Nekai. Welcome to my laboratory," says the bearded creature, turning toward you. "Keesa has explained that you are a friend from another planet."

"I'd like to help you fight the space dragons, if I can," you reply.

"Splendid! You couldn't have arrived at a better time."

Dr. Nekai takes one of the glass jars from the shelf. As he does, tiny points of light inside the jar sparkle like fireflies. He taps the glass bead on one end with his fingernail, producing a high musical note.

"This tone seems to attract the space dragons," he says. "Listen, you'll hear them."

Turn to page 44.

Dr. Nekai walks over to the wall and pulls down a map of Tambor.

"This is Shanar right here," he says, pointing to a spot on the map. "I've noted fire tracks made by the space dragons in their goings and comings. My guess is that their base is on the Rhegi Plateau, over here. I have a bad leg and cannot travel well. Besides, I must stay here and work to improve my acoustic bottles. Would you two be willing to look for the dragon base? If you can find it, I believe that together we can defeat them."

"I think it is our best hope," Keesa says, "but it is a hard journey. We must cross the Darblon Mountains."

"Please hurry," Dr. Nekai says, "before the space dragons destroy everything!"

You nod in assent. Your only question is whether you should go back to the life pod for more supplies before setting out on such a difficult journey.

If you set out immediately for the Darblon Mountains, turn to page 9.

If you decide to return first to the life pod for more supplies, turn to page 79.

"Yes," Keesa replies. "There have always been dragons on Tambor—dragons of flesh and blood. But the new ones from space are made of metal and crystal. They are worse than the hyskos—the terrible flying creatures that live high in the clouds of Tambor and swoop down to carry off and eat unwary Derns."

Keesa talks so fast you can hardly keep track of what he is saying.

"The space dragons just drove me back out of the ruins of Shanar, the city up ahead," he continues before you can even ask a question. "I was searching in the central library. There may be information there that will help me fight them. And our best scientist, Dr. Nekai, is working on a way to overcome them with sound power."

Turn to page 5.

You strap on your backpack and head out across the plain. You hike for what seems like hours. The structure in the distance barely gets closer. Suddenly the black spots reappear. You watch as they come toward you. As they get closer and bigger, you recognize them from pictures you've seen in books. They're dragons! with their huge, batlike wings, their hideous, scaled bodies, and orange-blue flames shooting from their mouths, there's no doubt about it. And you'd always thought dragons were mythical!

You dive to the ground. The dragons scream as they roar overhead, leaving a line of fire behind them. Your hair is scorched by the heat. Suddenly you see a hole in the ground—like a foxhole in a war zone, you think. You jump in and land a foot away from a creature about half your size. Except for a very large and pointed nose that takes up more than half his face, he could pass for small human. You look at him and then at your surroundings. You're inside a stone chamber. It is rectangular with roughly carved-out walls.

"Where are you from?" the creature asks in a high voice.

"I'm from—" you start. But you stop and stare at him in amazement. He's talking to you—and you can understand what he is saying!

Turn to page 4.

"I'd certainly feel safer underground," you say.

"Then follow me," Keesa replies, hurrying between two large piles of debris. "There should be a . . . Yes! Here it is!"

Keesa suddenly vanishes, and you run over to where he was standing. Sure enough, there's an opening in the ground. You try to lower yourself into it carefully, but you slip and find yourself sliding down a long chute. You land at the bottom with a thud.

"Ow!" you cry out. "My knee!"

"Are you badly hurt? Can you walk?" Keesa calls out from somewhere ahead in the darkness.

"I'm all right. I just skinned my knee," you call back.

"I shouldn't have gotten so far ahead," Keesa says, coming back to where you're sitting on the ground and nursing your knee.

"What do we do now?" you ask.

"We'll wait until our eyes get accustomed to the dim light," Keesa says. "Then we'll find out what's down here."

After a while, you and Keesa start moving again, down a long passageway. In many places the ceiling has caved in, and you have to climb over piles of rubble. You go on and on. You must be all the way to the edge of the city, or beyond it, you think. Then you see a bright light in the tunnel up ahead. Both of you hurry toward it. When you get there, you can only gape in amazement.

Keesa lets forth a squeal of delight. "What luck!"

Turn to page 14.

Keesa finds the beginning of the trail cut into the face of the cliff. He starts down. You try to follow close behind. The trail is hardly more than a series of footholds, clearly intended for someone Keesa's size. You haven't gone far when you realize how dangerous it is. You'd like to climb back up, but Keesa is already descending the cliff far below you.

You probe downward with your foot for each new foothold, trying to concentrate on one step at a time. After what seems like forever you reach the bottom.

Keesa is patiently sitting with his back against the base of the cliff. You rest for a while yourself, taking some food and drink from your pack and sharing it with Keesa. Then the two of you start out across the floor of the canyon.

You and Keesa wade across the shallow stream that flows along the rift. You clamber up onto dry land; you're happy not to have gotten wet much above the knees. Keesa doesn't seem to mind that he's soaked up to his neck. But ahead of you is the sheer face of a two-hundred-foot-high cliff.

"There *should* be a way up," Keesa says. "My guess is that we've gone too far south. If we head north along the base, we should eventually find a way to the top."

Turn to page 8.

Taking the footpath, you soon reach a ridge from which you can see a bleak valley spread out below. In the center of the valley, set near a peaceful stream, is a small house built of stone and clay—an adobe much like ones you've seen on Earth. Smoke is rising from the chimney. Your heart leaps. For the first time on this planet you have hopes of finding help!

Then you remember stories you've heard—experiences of desperate travelers on strange planets. The house, the stream, even the valley, may only be a mirage: an image made from your hopes, out of your longing for Earth. You head toward it anyway, expecting it to vanish at any moment. But the "mirage" stays put. It's real!

Cautiously, you walk up to the edge of the perfect circle of flowering plants surrounding the house. You reach in and pluck a fragrant roselike flower. This forbidding planet seems at once more friendly and welcoming. Looking more closely at the house, you almost jump out of your boots: A girl about your age is sitting in a rocking chair on the front porch.

Turn to page 29.

Within the hour you and Keesa have reached the magical city of Shanar. The buildings that haven't been destroyed by the dragons are shimmering, crystalline shapes—the most beautiful you've ever seen.

"Why do the dragons keep attacking the city?" you ask.

"That is one of the great mysteries about them," Keesa says. "We don't know."

You are threading your way through the debris when Keesa suddenly stops and listens.

"Quick! We must hide!" he whispers. "Something is coming toward us!"

You follow Keesa as he scampers behind a low, fire-blackened wall. Both of you crouch and listen. Somewhere, not far away, is the sound of many feet crunching along. As the sound comes closer, Keesa peeks through a crack in the wall. He gives a cry of surprise and stands up.

Turn to page 10.

You dive sideways and shield your eyes to keep from being cut by the flying glass. When you look around through the acrid smoke, you can't see anything but Keesa huddling beside you. All is quiet, except for the sound of electrical crackling and an occasional pop, delayed reaction to one of the shattered rods. Slowly the smoke clears. To your joy, all the robots are motionless. You work your way past the fallen robots and up the ramp, then into the tunnel. Peering into the cavern you see that the robots there are frozen in their places. The space dragons (which were never really alive) are dead!

Suddenly the lights begin to flicker.

"We'd better get out of here!" you say. "The power is going to go out at any minute."

You and Keesa dash back through the tunnel to the double doors. Fortunately, they're open. The wreck of a dragon lies just outside the entrance. It must have been about to enter when it went out of control.

You and Keesa run down the side of the mountain. You're both eager to tell Dr. Nekai and the other Derns to spread the word to all creatures hiding beneath the ground: The space dragons are dead. Tambor is free!

The End

The huge form of the Nedig looms close to you. Each of its hairs is as thick as a sapling. You see Keesa jump on the creature's back and grab hold of a hair. You do the same and suddenly find yourself rising up along the face of the cliff as if you were in a fast elevator. You hang on for dear life. After a while, a rock ledge appears in the mists—only a few feet away.

"Jump!" Keesa hollers as he springs onto the ledge.

You follow his instructions, but you don't jump as far as he did, so you're left dangling from the ledge as you hold on tightly with both hands. Keesa runs over and hauls you up onto the ledge. It's the first time you realize how strong he is for his size.

Turn to page 34.

You and Keesa follow the trail up the mountain. When you get above the tree line, you look back over the valley below. You see the scar of the Great Rift and, farther off on the horizon, the ruins of Shanar.

Then you see a black dot in the distance. It grows as you watch. You know at once it's a dragon. Fortunately, there are a number of crevices beside the trail. Quickly you and Keesa jump down into one.

As the dragon gets closer, a huge double door opens in the side of the mountain not far above you. The dragon roars by over your heads and sails through the open doors. Then they close. You continue climbing until you reach them.

"Let's hide among these bushes until the doors open," you tell Keesa.

It's not long before another dragon arrives. The doors swing open just above you, and the dragon flies inside. You and Keesa scramble up the mountain and scoot through the doors. A moment later they close behind you. You have entered the dragons' lair.

Turn to page 69.

When the girl sees you, she jumps up, almost as surprised as you are.

"You can't be real!" she exclaims. "I think I've been on this crazy planet too long. Now I'm seeing things!"

"I was thinking the same thing," you answer.

"Well, if you *are* real—and I still can't believe it—why don't you come up to the house?" she says. "There's a path just to the left of where you're standing."

Turn to page 60.

It doesn't take you long to find a narrow road going around the base of the mountain.

"This is very strange," Keesa says. "I've never seen a road like this. The way it's built up on the sides, it looks like some kind of track."

Following this road halfway around the mountain, you reach a huge semicircular door. The door is open and you peer cautiously through it into a dark tunnel. From somewhere deep within the mountain you can hear the hum of machinery.

"This is exciting!" Keesa says. "I think we've found an entrance to the dragon maintenance center. We won't have to climb the mountain."

You glance apprehensively at Keesa. "If that's so, it means this tunnel . . . may not be too good—"

Your words are interrupted by a roaring, rasping sound from behind. Turning, you confront one of the dragon monsters hurtling toward you. You hold out your acoustic bottle; but before you can tap it, it melts in a sheet of orange-blue flame.

The End

"Dragons?" you say. "You mean there are *dragons* on this planet?"

The girl nods. The smile leaves her face, and her eyes become moist. "Mother was killed by one last year. She was collecting firewood when it attacked. She didn't get back to the house in time. Now, I'm worried about Dad. He's been gone a long time and—"

The girl suddenly jumps up and points to a distant figure at the edge of the valley: a man limping and stumbling.

"There he is!" she exclaims. "And he looks as if he's hurt."

"We'll help him!" you call to the girl. You run down the garden path and out into the fire-scarred valley. By the time you reach the man, he has collapsed onto the ground. He's still conscious, but one leg is bleeding. You and the girl help him back to the house. When you get there, the two of you get him into bed.

"Much obliged to you, whoever you are," says the man, as the girl begins to wash and bandage his leg. "My daughter Millie and I are all alone now. We're at the end of our rope. Not much fuel left. The star charts said this was a water planet, but when we got here . . ." He smiles. "Thank goodness my leg isn't broken. I should be able to get around by tomorrow."

Turn to page 46.

You find a trail that winds up into the hills. The path is steep, and you're still weak from being in hibernation for so long. You stop to rest on a rock ledge. Looking out over the plain, your eyes open wide. Several perfect spheres are slowly rising from beyond the hills. They look like toy balloons, but they're so far away you know they must be much larger.

As you watch, fascinated, a flock of birds flies toward you. One of them separates from the rest. As it gets closer, you see that it's not a bird at all— it's a humanoid figure with wings! You strain to see whether the wings are actually part of its body.

The spheres continue to rise until they are lost from view. The bird-person swoops back toward his flock. They fly on, disappearing behind a hilltop. You wonder what other strange creatures exist on this planet.

The trail ahead of you branches in two directions. One branch is a footpath that looks as if it's been cut through the woods by human hands; the other branch leads over the hills, in the direction of the rising spheres.

If you follow the footpath, turn to page 22.

If you head toward the rising spheres, turn to page 76.

34

The Nedigs vanish into a cave in the cliff, the sound of their strange whistles receding into the distance.

"If I'm right," Keesa says, "this ledge will lead us to the top of the cliff."

You hike along the ledge, then gradually climb to the top. At last you find yourself on level ground. You and Keesa rest, then start off again, up the rocky slopes of the Rhegi Mountains.

After a few hours of hiking, you're at the base of the mountain. There's a trail leading straight up. Should you start climbing, or hike along the base and look for a pass?

If you go straight up the mountain, turn to page 28.

If you scout around the base first, turn to page 30.

You and Keesa flatten yourselves against the wall as the robots roll by. They don't appear to see you or know you're there. The new robots join the ones at the far end.

"We're lucky they're not programmed to notice intruders," you say, getting closer. Now you can see into an enormous room. Inside it, more robots are darting back and forth in front of a device that looks like an oversized xylophone. Long, vertical bars of glass or crystal are mounted in rows along the walls. Every few seconds, a robot strikes one of the bars with a long stick, and a musical note echoes down the corridor. On the far side is a ramp that you guess leads down to the dragon floor.

"This has to be the control room," you say excitedly. "Since they don't seem to notice us, maybe we can figure out how to take control."

Keesa shakes his head. "There are too many robots—and they're moving too fast. Let's skirt around them and continue on to the dragon floor."

If you go into the control room, turn to page 55.

If you agree with Keesa and go down to the dragon floor, turn to page 49.

Millie pulls the laser pistol out of her belt and aims it at the sky. A burst of pencil-thin laser light shoots up toward the beast. The dragon veers to one side in time to avoid being squarely hit, but a bright flash of light at the end of its tail indicates that it didn't escape the laser beam entirely. Seconds later, a piece of its tail breaks off and plummets to the ground. Then the dragon itself explodes in a shower of sparks!

"That'll teach them!" You pat your friend on the back.

But Millie's look tells you there's no cause for celebration. "We have to be more careful," she says. "They can sneak up on us like that."

You walk over and pick up one of the pieces of debris from the shattered dragon—a piece of metal. In the center of it there's a metal bolt.

"That's funny," you say. "This looks more like a piece from a spacecraft. I wonder . . ."

You feel Millie's hand on your elbow. "I wouldn't worry about that now. We've got more trouble. Look over there," she says, pointing to the south.

Turn to page 62.

You and Keesa stay on the ship. In an instant the door slams shut, and the dragon ship rises into the air.

You look out through the two circular windows in the front of the ship—they're probably what appear to be the "eyes" of the dragon from outside. Below, all the robots are running around in confusion. Suddenly you're thrown against the bulkhead as the ship tilts to a sharp angle, then shoots through the tunnel into the open sky.

You experiment with the bars, while desperately trying to control the ship. You soon learn that tapping one of the bars makes the ship go up, another down, and another sends a column of flame shooting out from the bow. You still have the acoustic bottle. You tap it. The dragon ship stops in midair! A bar on the control panel makes the ship do the same thing! And you find that the square box attached to the forward wall of the control room, between the "eyes" of the dragon, emits a series of "bongs" that programs the dragon ship through its destructive maneuvers. Computers do the rest. Now you're on your own—in control of a space dragon!

Turn to page 48.

You dive the dragon ship straight down. The acceleration takes your breath away. Looking out the porthole you see the mountain rushing up at you faster than you'd expected. You steer the ship away just in time to keep from hitting the mountain, but then you have to prepare for another crisis: The other dragon ships are closing in fast.

You try to maneuver, but you're too late. The dragon ships crash into you and each other simultaneously. All of the ships are blown to bits with a force so great that the dragon tunnel caves in; the rest of the dragons are buried forever. It's too bad that no one will ever know it was you who saved Tambor.

The End

"Let's go for the deuterium," you tell Millie.

"According to Dad, it will take us two Earth days to get there, extract the deuterium, and get back here," she says.

"What do you mean by Earth days?" you ask. "Is time on this planet measured differently?"

"The days here are a little over two Earth days long," she says. "If we leave at dawn tomorrow, with luck we can find the water and the deuterium and get back here before darkness sets in. Unfortunately, dragons aren't our only problem. There are many dangerous creatures still alive on this planet, and most of them come out in the dark."

Millie serves you a meal of fresh salad and vegetables from her garden, and after dinner you settle down to sleep. When you wake up, much refreshed, Millie has everything packed and ready to go. She says good-bye to her father, then the two of you leave the safety of the house and its force shield and head out across the desolate valley.

"I have a map that my father gave me," Millie says. "I also have his laser pistol. The charge in it is low, but it should have a couple of shots left."

Turn to page 59.

But as you close in on Parau, you begin to notice that it's not a moon at all.

"Why that's a space station!" you exclaim.

You fly the ship around the space station and locate a large, open port. You're able to pilot the dragon ship through it. A huge door closes silently behind you.

You're excited to have discovered a space station, but your hopes fall as you cruise through it. There is no sign of life anywhere. Then, looking up, you see the great space door opening again. A huge ship is entering. Your heart leaps as you recognize its type. And even at this distance you can see the large Earth flag painted on its hull. You're about to be rescued!

The End

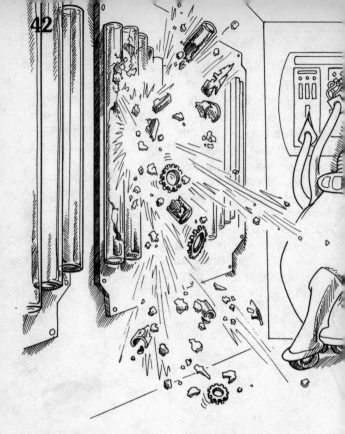

Keesa quickly throws his gears—and misses the glass bars completely. You take more careful aim. The first gear glances off harmlessly. The next one shatters three glass bars in a row! You're blinded by a bright flash of energy. The whole control panel starts to explode, filling the room with showers of sparks and flying fragments of glass.

Turn to page 25.

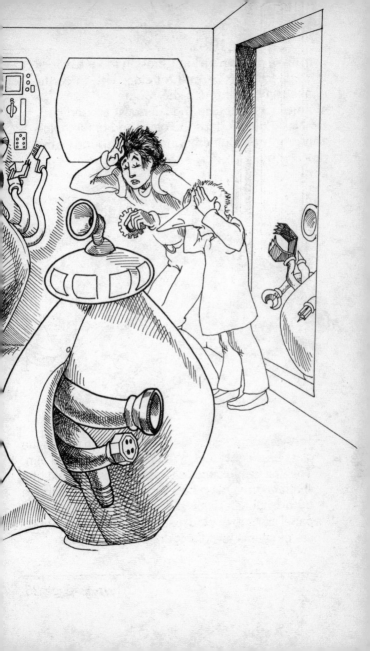

In a few moments a loud, crashing sound comes from directly above, and a tremor like an earthquake rumbles through the room.

Small bits of the ceiling fall down around you. Dr. Nekai quickly taps the other end of the bottle and produces a different note. The sound of the dragons quickly ends.

Turn to page 3.

You and Keesa follow the riverbed for hours. As you trudge along, you notice a small black dot high in the sky. Then the dot starts getting larger.

"Keesa—a dragon!" you shout.

You look up in horror as the dark shape plummets toward you.

"The bottle!" Keesa yells. But you are already holding it above your head. You tap it again and again. You hear the weird vibrating tone that Dr. Nekai produced in his laboratory. The dragon swerves and, to your great relief, flies off at great speed.

Keesa smiles. "Thank goodness! But we must hurry. If more than one dragon comes . . ."

You and Keesa continue on at an even faster pace. Soon you reach the edge of a cliff overlooking a huge natural chasm. It looks about half a mile deep and almost as much across. The other side is barely visible through the thick mist that's rising from the chasm.

"This is the Great Rift," Keesa says. "Normally there would be a tremendous waterfall tumbling into the river below. But because of the recent dryness on the planet, it's only a trickle. There's a very narrow trail that leads down the face of the cliff and up the other side. But it might be better if we headed south. Eventually, the rift becomes much narrower, and there's a natural bridge across it."

If you go down the face of the cliff, turn to page 21.

If you go south, turn to page 63.

"You'd better rest a while, Dad," Millie says, motioning to you to follow her into the other room.

"What we need most is deuterium fuel," Millie says when the two of you are alone. "But it can only be extracted from large amounts of water. Our fuel is so low now, we won't be able to generate the force shield against the dragons much longer."

Suddenly, a siren goes off behind the house.

"The dragon alarm!" Millie cries as she dashes into another room. "I must activate the shield."

You run out onto the front porch. Flying low across the floor of the valley are three black shapes approaching at a high speed. Just before they swoop over the house, a dome of sparkling light surrounds the house and the gardens. You can see now that the beasts overhead are indeed dragons. Long, flickering orange flames shoot out from their mouths! The flames engulf the dome and the area surrounding it. But the force shield holds—the little house and garden are untouched!

Turn to page 74.

"What'll we do now that we have our own dragon?" Keesa asks with a laugh.

"Maybe we can use it to destroy the other dragons," you say.

"We're very much outnumbered."

"That's true," you say with a smile, "but don't you see—generally these dragons are programmed to do only a limited number of tasks, such as attacking and destroying things on the ground and going back and forth to the repair base. We can be much smarter."

"Watch out!" Keesa yells. "Look out the porthole!"

A long string of dragons is coming toward you.

"Can we outrun them?" Keesa asks.

"No, but we can outdodge them," you answer grimly.

You throw the ship into an upward loop at maximum speed. You swoop in a half-circle and come back down, close behind the last dragon in the column. "Fire!" you yell at Keesa.

Turn to page 73.

You and Keesa ease your way down the ramp that leads to the dragon floor. When you finally get close to the dragons, you gasp at the sight of these huge mechanical monsters sculptured to look like dragons. You realize at once what evil weapons of destruction they are. When you get over your initial shock, you notice the open ports in their sides and see that their insides resemble those of spaceships.

Suddenly a dragon roars into the cavern and settles gracefully to the floor at the end of the dragon line closest to you. A door in its side opens downward and becomes a ramp. Two of the robots roll up the ramp and enter the dragon ship. A few minutes later, they exit. You and Keesa quickly run up the ramp and into the dragon.

You go forward to the control room and find smaller versions of the glass rods you saw in the control room. You tap one of the bars. An engine roars to life somewhere on the ship.

If you get off the ship, turn to page 52.

If you stay inside the ship, turn to page 38.

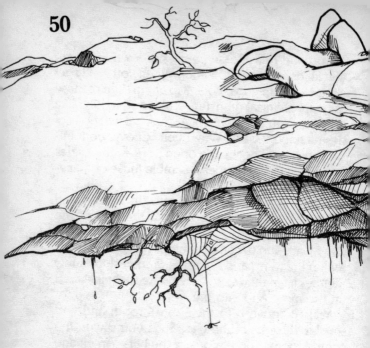

You get to the center without any difficulty—
then suddenly your foot slips. You barely have
time to throw your arms around the arch and hang
on. The acoustic bottle and your bag of supplies go
flying off into the deep ravine below. Keesa throws
himself flat on the arch and reaches down to help
you. With his help, you manage to pull yourself
back. But before you have a chance to breathe a
sigh of relief, you see a dragon diving down on
you.

Turn to page 81.

You tap Keesa on the shoulder. "Let's get out of here."

The two of you dash for the door. You make it through just as the outside ramp starts to fold back into the side of the ship. As you leap to the ground, you see a robot rolling toward you.

"Watch out!" you yell at Keesa. At the same time, you dive out of the robot's path. But suddenly steel pincers are picking you up. The robot has mistaken you for a repair part. He holds you aloft as he rolls toward a dragon. You struggle to get free. The robot reacts, tightening its grip, tighter . . . tighter.

The End

You find yourselves in a small room. There's a door at the other side that leads to a ramp, spiraling down to somewhere below.

"Those robots on the floor below look as if they're moving on wheels," Keesa says. "They probably use ramps instead of stairways."

"I hope they don't use this one very often," you say, "because I want to go down it and have a look."

When you and Keesa reach the bottom of the ramp, you find a long corridor. At the far end of it you catch sight of robots hurrying back and forth.

"Let's get closer and see exactly what they're doing," you whisper.

The two of you tiptoe out into the corridor and head toward the robots. You haven't gone far when you see another group of robots speeding down the corridor from the other direction. You realize you can't get back to the ramp in time. You're trapped between two groups of robots!

Turn to page 35.

54

"I think it's snoring," you say.

Millie's father laughs nervously.

At last the fuel gauges register a full tank. Millie's father gives the command, the rockets roar to life, and the ship slowly lifts off the back of the tremendous creature. The ship's thrusters sear the monster's back, and it rears up like a volcano erupting, snapping at the rising ship with its gigantic jaws.

Turn to page 80.

You and Keesa make your way into the control room. You're soon surrounded by robots, but they are unaware of your presence, so you're able to dodge them. Watching them, you learn that the glass bars on the "xylophone" are used to direct the takeoffs and landings of the dragons as well as preparing them for repair and maintenance on the floor below.

"This may be our chance," you whisper to Keesa. "If we smash their control apparatus, we can ground all the dragons—permanently!"

"I'm for that," Keesa says. "But how do we do it?"

"I noticed a small pile of metal parts just outside the door to this room," you say. "We'll smash the glass bars on the xylophone."

You and Keesa weave your way through the robots and back to the door. You each take one of the round, gearlike parts in each hand.

"Now!" you shout.

Turn to page 42.

You land on the dragon's head, just above the hump between its eyes. Hoping to knock out its sensors, you raise your spear and plunge it down.

You were right in thinking you had found the dragon's sensors. The only trouble is that it used them to sense *you*! With a jerk of its head the beast sends out a long tongue of orange-blue flame— and a moment later, there's nothing left of you but falling cinders!

The End

You brace yourself and send the ship almost straight up at top speed. You're pressed so hard against the wall of the control room that you almost black out. Up and up the ship climbs, and you can't reach the controls!

Suddenly, the engine cuts out. Everything is silent. You realize you're weightless!

Keesa floats toward you. "There's our planet 'way down there!"

You float closer to the window.

"We've gone into orbit," you say. "We're in space!"

In a few minutes Tambor looks no larger than the Earth looks from the moon. As you get closer to the window, you spot another globe off to the side of your ship. It looks much larger than Tambor.

"What's that on our left?" you ask Keesa.

"That could be Parau," he says. "It's one of Tambor's moons—the smallest."

"Whatever it is," you say, "we're drifting rapidly toward it. We've got to get the propulsion mechanism of this ship working again, or we'll crash!"

Turn to page 94.

The two of you follow a trail that winds first through rolling meadows, then through hilly scrubland.

"Did animals make these trails?" you ask Millie. "They're a lot wider than the animal trails on Earth."

"Dragons," she replies.

The two of you trudge along in silence. You hike for hours.

"All these hills look alike," you say. "I hope we're going in the right direction."

Millie stops short and looks around as if trying to get her bearings. "I've come this far before with Dad to help him search for half-burned logs that still had some usable wood left in them. That's how he built the house. We dragged them home, and he used a laser saw to cut the logs into lumber."

"Let's rest a bit," you say.

Millie stops and puts down the deuterium extractor. You let the two bags—your knapsack and the one that Millie packed—drop to the ground. You both sit down on the ground and lean back against a large, charred log.

Millie leans 'way back with her hands behind her head and looks up at the sky. Suddenly, she jumps back to her feet. A great metallic gray dragon is almost on top of you!

Turn to page 37.

You still can't believe it, but you find the path and head toward the girl. Your spirits rise further—and your mouth waters—as you pass rows of succulent vegetables growing on both sides of the path.

You climb the steps to the porch.

"I'm from planet Earth," you say, feeling a bit foolish.

"I am too," the girl replies in a matter-of-fact tone, as if Earth visitors passed by all the time. "How did you get here?"

"I was marooned here when my life pod crashed," you say, "and—"

"So were we!" she exclaims. "We came in a small spaceship. It's out behind the house. My father was a space engineer back on Earth. He got a job with the Vorks on some strange planet. He took us, Mother and me, that is, with him. But we all got so homesick that the Vorks gave us a spaceship with a built-in force shield against meteorites and enough deuterium fuel to get home. Dad got lost or something on the way to Earth and we ended up here. We don't have enough fuel left to get back to Earth—just enough to activate our force shield when the dragons attack."

Turn to page 31.

Again and again you tap the bottle. Loud as it is, your ears can stand it, so beautiful are the tones and overtones making up the harmonic pulse of sound. You can only compare it to a chord played on a great organ.

The hyskos fly out in all directions to survey the effects of Dr. Nekai's bottle. In a few hours the reports come back: Everywhere, the dragons are dropping from the sky. Peace has come again to Tambor.

The End

A huge gray curtain seems to be sweeping across the hills in your direction. Brilliant flashes of lightning fill the sky.

Millie's face pales. "It's a death storm!"

"What do we do?" you ask.

"According to my father's map, there should be a number of caves somewhere up ahead. If we can reach them, we'll be safe, but I'm not sure we can."

"I have a light nylon tent in my pack," you say. "It will give us some protection!"

Millie looks at you uncertainly.

*If you say, "Let's run for the caves,"
turn to page 100.*

*If you say, "Let's set up the tent,"
turn to page 95.*

You and Keesa follow along the edge of the rift. You're careful not to get too close to the edge. The rift, as Keesa warned, gradually gets narrower. But up ahead you can see a natural stone arch stretching all the way across it.

"Will the arch really hold our weight?" you ask. "It looks very narrow and fragile in the center. And what if we get caught by a dragon when we're halfway across?"

"Don't worry," Keesa says. "That arch has been there for thousands of years, I've been told, and many have gone across it. And we still have the acoustic bottle to protect us from the dragons."

"You're right. I don't know what I'm worrying about," you say as you start across, with Keesa right behind you.

Turn to page 50.

You leave the boat behind and head along the shore. As you follow the lake around the curving shoreline, you're alarmed to find the beach littered with bones. Mostly they look like fish bones, but some look like the bones of Derns!

Suddenly, you hear a crunching sound behind you. You turn to see a huge snake slithering up the beach. You try to run, but another great snake blocks the way. You see others swimming toward you, and when you turn the beach is full of them!

Your bones are soon added to those on the beach.

The End

You hold up your light and gaze into the darkness. The light reflects on the water. Millie takes out her extractor and drops the intake hose into the water.

"My sensor registers positive for deuterium!"

Millie hugs you excitedly and then returns to her instrument. "It will take a while to collect the amount we need," she says.

"Well, that'll give the storm time to pass," you reply.

Hours later, the two of you emerge from the cave with all the deuterium you need. The sky has cleared, and you set out at once for Millie's house.

You arrive just as darkness is falling. You gasp at the sight before you, horrified by what you see. The house and the garden are a wreck. The garden was blown away in the storm. So was most of the roof. Millie's father stands on what is left of the front porch.

"We ran out of fuel, and the shield went down just as the storm struck," he calls. "At least the dragons haven't been back. Maybe the storm—"

But he has no time to finish his sentence. Millie runs forward and hugs him, while she breathlessly tells him how you found a new supply of fuel. The three of you run to the spaceship behind the house. Millie's father transfers the fuel to the rocket engines, and a moment later they respond noisily. You settle into your seats and then lift off from Tambor and start your journey back to Earth.

Turn to page 71.

You take the hole on the right. After going through a few more chambers, you reach a huge cavern. Inside is an enormous lake that stretches almost as far as you can see.

You walk along the shore for a while. Then, to your surprise, you come upon a rowboat that's pulled up on the shore. There are two oars in the bottom of the boat.

Where is the settlement of the Derns that Keesa was talking about? you wonder. Is it somewhere along the shore, or is it on the other side of the lake?

*If you continue along the shore,
turn to page 64.*

If you take the boat and head out across the lake, turn to page 114.

As your eyes get used to the faint light, you see that the tunnel you're in has been hewn out of solid rock and blackened by the fire of dragons' breath.

You hear the hum of machinery, growing louder as you proceed. The tunnel gently curves for a few hundred yards and then comes to an abrupt end.

You look down a hundred feet at an amazing scene. On the wide, circular floor far below, the dragons are lined up in orderly rows. Robots are moving around them like workers on an assembly line. There are open ports in the sides of the dragons, and some of the robots are going in and out, like ants streaming in and out of ant hills.

You and Keesa stand there spellbound. But you're startled into action by the sound of the doors to the mountain opening behind you. Another dragon is coming in—and you're right in its path!

"Flatten yourself against the wall," you yell at Keesa, as you run to one side of the tunnel.

When you reach the wall, you notice a thin, curving line and push against it. A section of the wall swings open, and you and Keesa jump through—just as the dragon roars past.

Turn to page 53.

You thank Keesa and start into the passageway leading to an underground tunnel. "Make sure you take the right hole," he calls out as he starts climbing a rope up to the surface.

When you reach the tunnel you're dismayed to see how narrow it is. You'll have to crawl. The tunnel leads to another chamber. There is another hole in this chamber that leads to still *another* chamber.

Luckily, the phosphorescent walls glow just enough for you to make your way along.

Soon you begin to wish you'd gone with Keesa to the city. The series of chambers seems endless. At last you come to one that has two holes besides the one you came in through. Now what do I do? you wonder. There's no clue to help you make a choice, except for Keesa's words: "Make sure you take the right hole."

You try to figure out what Keesa meant by the "right" hole. Did he mean the hole on the "right"? The one to the right is small—barely big enough to squeeze through—and it looks dusty and unused. The one to the left is large enough so you don't even have to stoop to enter it.

You stop to think. Maybe the left hole is the "right" hole!

If you go through the hole on the left, turn to page 110.

If you go through the hole to the right, turn to page 67.

Three months have passed since you, Millie, and her father set out for Earth. You are now passing the Alcor star system. Traveling at two-thirds the speed of light, you should arrive on Earth in just twenty-six days.

You expected Millie's father to be excited and happy, now that you're so close to your goal. Instead, he looks strained and nervous. You're standing at the starboard window admiring the six beautiful ringed planets of Alcor. "Anything wrong?" you ask.

He slowly shakes his head. "I can't bear to tell Millie. We've been using more deuterium than I'd calculated—chances are we won't have braking power adequate for entering Earth's atmosphere."

"Any way we can get more deuterium?" you ask.

Millie's father shakes his head. "Not unless we land on Alcor's water planet. Space Advisory lists it as unsafe for landing. But . . . I'll try it if you're willing."

If you decide to land on the water planet, turn to page 2.

If you decide to continue traveling directly to Earth, turn to page 106.

As you reach the gates of the city you see a huge dragon hovering there. It looks as if it's waiting for you. Your tympor dodges to the left. The dragon can't move as quickly as the tympor. Not even a lion or tiger can move as quickly as a tympor. If the predator had been a lion or a tiger, the tympor would have made it. But dragons are able to shoot jets of flame.

The End

The little Dern acts quickly. A burst of flame shoots from the mouth of your ship and engulfs the back end of the dragon ahead of you. Its controls literally melt away, and the dragon dives toward the ground. But you don't have long to congratulate yourself—the other dragons soon peel off in different directions and start the same looping maneuver you just performed. Suddenly they're all coming at you!

"Those dragons must be programmed to learn from experience," you say to Keesa. "We've got to do something fast!"

If you try to gain altitude, turn to page 58.

*If you go into a high-speed dive,
turn to page 39.*

Millie returns from the shield controls. "That was close!" she says. "They give us so little warning time these days."

"I have an idea," you say. "Do you have any small, workable cadmium batteries in your spaceship?"

"Maybe one or two," she says. "Why?"

"I have a long-range rescue-beam generator in my life pod," you say. "Its battery was damaged when I crashed. I can go back, replace the battery, and reactivate it. There must be somebody out there in this part of the galaxy who can rescue us."

"I have another idea," Millie says. "We have a deuterium extractor. What we need is a large body of water. Dad found an underground lake not too far from here. If you would help me find it . . ."

If you go back to the life pod for the rescue beam generator, turn to page 98.

If you go in search of the deuterium, turn to page 40.

The hyskos are waiting for you. One of them carries you, and another carries the bottle, back to their city in the sky.

"This device will get rid of the dragons," you say, "but I'll only show you how to use it if you promise to stop eating the Derns."

"We will try to do without them," says the leader of the hyskos. "Actually, since they've been so scarce, we've had to learn to eat other foods. They are now just a very rare delicacy."

"If you ring this end," you explain to the hyskos, "and tap the bottle—"

The note that sounds is much louder than you expected; it pulses hypnotically through the air . . .

Turn to page 61.

Following the path toward the spheres, you reach a ridge that overlooks a broad, muddy swamp. It's different from anything you've ever seen on Earth. A huge bubble is rising out of the water. Actually it isn't a bubble at all, but a large, glistening sphere that suddenly breaks free of the ground and floats upward—just like the ones you saw before.

While you're watching the sphere, you sense a presence behind you. Turning, you see several birdlike creatures with humanoid features. They all have spears aimed at your throat.

One of them grabs you with his long, clawed feet. You feel a rush of wind as the creature flaps its wings. Suddenly you're in the air. You rise higher as he beats his powerful wings! You look down in terror as the ground retreats below. The birdman has you in an iron grip. You have no reason to think he will drop you—still, you can't look anymore, so you close your eyes.

The birdman is coming in for a landing. You open your eyes and see a broad platform. It's built on top of a group of spheres—the same kind you saw rise from the swamp. At the center is a village made up of winglike tents held together by long filaments of some sort.

Turn to page 99.

78

The ship carries a long hose for the fuel collector. You hop down onto the back of the monster and pull the hose behind you until you reach the water. It takes several hours for the collector to extract and refine the precious deuterium from the water. Meanwhile, the three of you wait anxiously, knowing that nothing more than a sneeze could spell your doom. Every once in a while, a horrible, rasping roar comes from the monster's snout.

Turn to page 54.

The dragons above have stopped their attack. You and Keesa say good-bye to Dr. Nekai, and he gives you the acoustic bottle to take with you. After a few hours' trek you reach the wreckage of your life pod. Keesa is fascinated by the strange craft, but while he is examining it, he lets out a scream and starts running back toward the plain.

"Come back! What's the mat—" you start.

A blow on the back of your head stops you short. Dr. Nekai's acoustic bottle flies out of your hand and crashes to the ground. The next moment you feel yourself being lifted up into the air. Your last thought before you black out is: I've been captured by the dragons!

Turn to page 113.

Millie's father navigates your spaceship through space, away from the hideous sea monster and toward the solar system. One day you wake up from your sleep period and peer out the view screen. You let out a whoop. You're looking at the planet Earth itself, growing larger every second. And there were times you thought you'd never see it again. . . .

The End

You go to the right, following a narrow, twisting passageway leading to a descending staircase, and cautiously you start down. When you reach the bottom, you're in a large, circular chamber. On the other side of the chamber are dragons! They stare at you with blazing eyes. You stand frozen, afraid to move. But as you stare at them, you realize that these dragons are different from the ones up above. They are much smaller, hardly bigger than you. And there's a gentle look in their eyes.

You smile for the first time in a long time.

Suddenly, a Dern appears from somewhere at the side of the chamber. He looks something like Keesa but seems to be younger.

"Try not to scare them," he says.

"What are these dragons doing here?" you ask.

"Ever since the metal dragons arrived from space, the native dragons have hid underground. I am trying to take care of them so that one day, when the evil dragons are gone, these kindly dragons can return to the surface. They are part of our legends and tales."

As if to say that he trusts you, one of the dragons trots over and licks your hand. At that moment you know that the space dragons will be defeated and that someday all will be well again on the planet.

The End

84

You and Keesa run down the street as fast as you can, trying to avoid tripping over the debris scattered about. The tympors gallop on ahead.

"I have an idea," says Keesa. He lets out a shrill, strange cry. Several of the tympors stop in their tracks. Keesa utters some more sounds, and two of them trot back to where you are.

"Quick! Jump on!" Keesa says, giving you a boost up onto the neck of one of them. "Hold tight! They move fast!"

Keesa mounts the other one, and the tympors dash forward.

The dragons are already pouring flames into the streets behind you.

Turn to page 72.

"I could never do this on Earth," you say to yourself, and realize at once that such a thing is possible here only because Tambor has such light gravity.

It takes a long time, but gradually you get your wings under control. Sarda beckons you to land on a platform. There she sits with you and tells you why the hyskos wanted you to be one of them.

"A strange race of alien dragons invaded this planet of Tambor some time ago. We have never learned where they came from or why they came here. We only know that they have driven the animals we prey on underground, where we can't reach them. So far we have not been able to defeat the dragons. We need new ideas. We know you come from space. You must know how to fight the dragons. You can help us."

Another hysko lands on your platform. He speaks in a rasping voice to Sarda. She nods, then turns to you. "The dragons have come. It's time to attack!"

Turn to page 112.

You drop down in front of the dragon's mouth. If it breathes fire at this moment, you'll be cooked in midair. But you drive your spear into the dragon's throat anyway. Its engine sputters—you've jammed the intake valve! A few seconds later, the mechanical monster plummets silently to the ground.

The hyskos now know how to defeat the dragons. It's only a matter of time before all the artificial dragons are destroyed.

That evening, back at the city in the air, the hyskos award you every honor they have. It's a wonderful celebration. Tomorrow will be soon enough to think about getting back to Earth.

The End

You find the stairway that leads back to the surface. You poke your head out and peer cautiously around.

The broad plain stretches before you, with the Darblon Mountains in the distance beyond. Parts of the plain are fairly rough. If you run from crevice to crevice and keep a low profile, you think, the hyskos probably won't spot you.

Turn to page 89.

You start **across the plain, but before you've** gone far, the dark shadow of a hysko falls across you. It swoops down toward you—will the hysko attack you or does it want to help you?

Suddenly it doesn't matter: A larger shadow falls across the ground—that of a dragon! Seconds later, a blast of flame finishes you—and the hysko too.

The End

Millie's father steers the ship closer, while you apply braking thrusters. Through the port you can see that the island has an odd shape. Then you watch waves ripple from one end to the other.

"There's something very strange and unnatural about that island," you say. "I thought I saw it move. Do you think it could be some kind of monster?"

But no one answers your question. Instead, you all stare, transfixed, as the tail of the island wiggles again, sending another rash of waves along its side.

"How gently can we land this ship?" you ask.

"We'll find out in a minute," Millie's father answers, working the controls to bring the ship into a slow, looping glide.

He sets the ship down gracefully and gently on the great creature's back. The whole ship vibrates wildly as the beast quivers. Then all is still.

"It's as if a fly landed on the back of an elephant," Millie says.

"Let's hope we can keep from tickling it," you say.

Turn to page 78.

Your knowledge that hydrogen can be a very potent explosive gives you an idea. "Tell them I have to go back to where they captured me," you say.

Keesa speaks to the hyskos in their own language.

"They say that it's all right for you do so, but that you will be closely guarded," Keesa says. "They say that I must stay here."

One of the hyskos picks you up and flies back to your life pod. Several others follow. You crawl inside the pod and search around for something that can be used as a fuse. You find a large cloth sheet and tear it up into thin strips. You also find a small, old-fashioned flint lighter from Earth.

You get all these things together, and when you come out again, the hyskos carry you back to Keesa.

"Tell them," you say to Keesa, "that whenever there's a dragon below, they must puncture a yarya so enough of the gas escapes for it to fall straight down. At the same time, they must attach one of these strips of cloth and light it with this lighter. When the cloth burns to the skin of the yarya, the yarya will explode and destroy the dragon. They can bomb the dragons out of the sky."

Turn to page 103.

"I'll become a hysko," you say. "Will I learn to fly?"

"Yes, and you'll learn to love it," says the bird-woman. "I, Sarda, will teach you myself."

Sarda goes back into one of the tents and comes out again with two sets of wings and harnesses, one smaller than the other.

"This small set we use for children. Even though you are no longer a child, it will fit you better," she says.

The two birdwomen fit you into the elaborate harness.

"Now," Sarda says. "It's time."

"Can't I take a course or something first?" you protest. "I haven't the slightest idea what to do."

"You will," says Sarda. "Just do what I do. Come on. Follow me."

She walks over to the edge of the platform, extends her wings with her arms, and sails off into the sky. You go to the edge and step off. You find yourself plummeting straight down.

Sarda is quickly there, her wings folded, falling beside you.

"Extend your arms like this," she calls.

She spreads her wings and glides away smoothly. You struggle to do the same, fighting against the tremendous pull on your arms. Finally, you get your arms extended and are able to fly behind Sarda. You try moving your arms up and down—and find yourself soaring up into the sky. It's exciting. It's wonderful!

Turn to page 85.

You and Keesa pull yourselves along to the controls.

"This looks like a modified space drive," you say. "Maybe we can really convert this dragon to a full-performance spaceship."

"Don't ask me," Keesa says.

You try to remember what the Taurons taught you. You switch some wires. The space-drive engine hums—the gauges on the panel indicate it's operational and ready.

"Now that we can maneuver, I'm going to land on that moon of yours and try to figure out what to do from there," you tell Keesa.

Turn to page 41.

You and Millie quickly unpack the tent and set it up. You try to anchor it to the ground as firmly as you can. You're able to crawl inside only seconds before the storm arrives.

The storm is a very bad one, as "death storms" always are. The tent, with you and Millie inside, is swept up by the gale and blown for almost a mile before being deposited in the deep gully that becomes your grave.

The End

Then you see one of the bird-people flying up from below. He holds Keesa in his talonlike hands.

The birdman carrying Keesa lands next to you and drops him at your feet.

"Keesa!" you exclaim. "What are these creatures?"

"They are the hyskos!" Keesa exclaims. "Predators of the sky. They even kill us Derns for food. At least I can use their language."

Keesa looks at the hyskos and gives a series of grunts. They reply with the same kind of sounds.

Keesa explains. "They say there are so few Derns left on the surface of Tambor that they can no longer survive. I can't say I have much sympathy for them, since I'm a Dern myself. They say the dragons must be destroyed so the Derns will return to the surface in large numbers. If we help them get rid of the dragons, they will let *us* live."

"But what can we do to help?" you ask.

Keesa translates your question to the hyskos.

"They need a weapon of some sort," Keesa says. "Their spears don't affect the dragons."

Turn to page 104.

You make it safely back to your life pod and insert the cadmium battery in the emergency beacon. Instantly, the monitor shows that your signal is being sent into space at the speed of light. Space is so vast, you know that no patrol ship from Earth will receive the message for years. Your only hope is that friendly aliens patroling nearby will pick it up and come to your rescue.

You set out to return to Millie and her father. With your help perhaps they can hold out against the dragons. Maybe, like certain plagues that have visited Earth, the dragons will die out in time. At least now you have the hope of rescue.

The End

The birdman sets you down in an open space at the middle of the strange village in the sky. A birdwoman walks toward you from the nearest tent. She tries to talk to you in a language of grunts, but you can't understand any of it.

"I'm from the planet Earth, and I crashed here on this planet and . . ." you say without much hope of being understood.

The birdwoman turns and heads for another tent. A few minutes later she comes back with another birdwoman who stares intently into your eyes.

"Now I have it," she says. "Your language is very difficult but some of us hyskos have mastered the art of speaking through another creature's mind. I can say no more until you decide if you will become one of us . . . or return to the ground."

Become a hysko? you think. Does that mean I'll have to fly? You'd like to go back to the ground, but it might be safer to play along with them for the moment.

*If you decide to become a hysko,
turn to page 93.*

*If you decide to return to the ground,
turn to page 108.*

100

Millie grabs the extractor and you both start running toward the caves. You decide to leave the heavy pack behind and come back for it later.

"According to the map," Millie calls to you, "the caves are at the other end of this narrow valley."

The storm whirls across the meadow. A huge black cloud towers over the land. Your eyes are almost blinded by the brilliant flashes of light as the front bears down on you.

"There's a cave up ahead! I see it!" Millie shouts.

You see it, too, and together you dive into the entrance just as the storm thunders by. The wind lashes rain into the cave, and you retreat far to the back, while holding your flashlight in front of you.

In the very depths of the cave you see a tunnel leading downward. Cautiously you descend, with Millie a step behind. At the bottom, the stairway opens out onto a ledge. And just below the ledge is the smooth surface of a body of water!

"What luck!" Millie exclaims. "This is an entrance to the lake—an entrance we didn't know about—and it's much closer to our house!"

Turn to page 66.

The hyskos fly you back to Shanar and help you find the underground entrance to the realm of the Derns. To make sure you don't escape, they stand guard while you try to find Dr. Nekai.

You remember the way well enough from your previous visit, but when you finally reach Dr. Nekai's laboratory, you find it in a shambles. Most of his bottles are broken, and the inside of the laboratory has been ravaged by fire. What could have happened? There's no way the hyskos or dragons could have passed through the narrow tunnels leading to the refuge of the Derns.

In the midst of a pile of broken glass you spy a note—no more than a series of strange symbols—the written language of the Derns. Beneath the writing is a mazelike diagram that could show the route to where Dr. Nekai has gone.

There seems little doubt that Dr. Nekai was fleeing still another predator on this unfortunate planet. Should you follow the diagram and try to find him? Or should you go back to the surface and face the hyskos?

If you try to find Dr. Nekai, turn to page 109.

If you return to the surface, turn to page 87.

Keesa explains it all to the hyskos.

At first the hyskos don't believe your plan will work, but after they've destroyed the first few dragons, you and Keesa became their heroes.

The hyskos have gone so long without the Derns for food that in desperation they've turned to a number of edible plants to stay alive. They realize now that they like their new food just as much. But you teach the Derns how to make and shoot bows and arrows to fight off the hyskos, just in case the hyskos revert to their old ways. The Derns are so grateful that they elect you their new grand emperor.

The End

104

"I think they smashed their best bet when they made me drop my acoustic bottle back at the life pod," you say.

"We'll have to think of something else," Keesa says.

"What's this thing we're sitting on?" you ask.

"It's a yarya—a plant that grows in the only swamp left on Tambor. They expand and fill with hydrogen as they grow. When they are full grown, they break loose and float up into the air. The hyskos gather them to form floating villages high in the sky. For some reason the dragons never bother them up here."

You have an idea—actually two ideas. The first involves going back to your life pod; the other is to go back to the city and try to find the professor again.

If you tell the hyskos you have to go back to the life pod, turn to page 91.

If you say you must go back to Shanar, turn to page 102.

You gaze at the strange landscape about you. Not far away is a range of low hills. They face a vast plain stretching to the horizon. The countryside is very beautiful, except for one thing: The hills and meadows are crisscrossed with ugly black streaks, as if they'd been raked by a blowtorch.

Something on the horizon, far across the plain, catches your eye. Though it's tiny from this distance, it's clearly a geometric structure. It must have been built by intelligent life. As you watch, several black dots bound up and down in the air above the structure. Several flashes of red light appear along its side, and then a cloud of smoke rises from it. What's causing this strange display? you wonder. It almost looks as if someone's fighting a battle. A few seconds later you hear a distant rumble.

Turn to page 13.

Precisely twenty-five days later, you enter the solar system. The ship's braking thrusters are applied.

"We'll need every drop of fuel for landing," Millie's dad says. "That is, if there's any fuel left. These gauges aren't too accurate."

You sleep fitfully that night. Not long after you've finally fallen asleep, you're awakened by Millie's voice: "Come on!"

You leap out of your bunk. The planet Earth fills the entire view screen. You help with the small thruster rockets that turn the ship's stern toward the planet. Then the main rocket engine roars back to life—using the tiny bit of fuel left. The ship settles down through the atmosphere and shifts from rockets to jets for the final landing.

You hear the jets sputtering during the final descent.

An alarm sounds.

"LOSS OF POWER," the audio warning announces.

"Deploy parachutes!" you yell at the computer. *CRASH!*

You're out cold.

Turn to page 117.

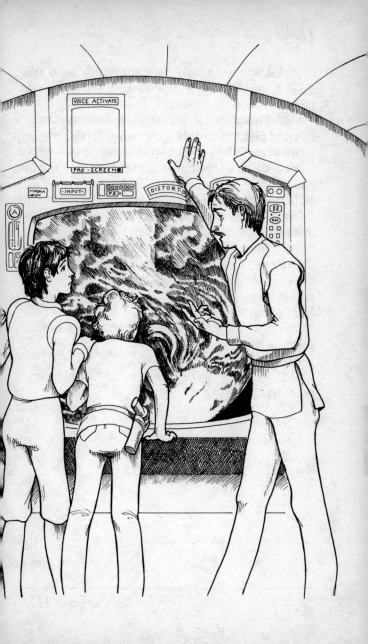

"I'd rather go back to the ground," you say.

"Then back to the ground it is," the birdwoman says in a hard voice.

She goes back into the tent. A few seconds later, two of the male hyskos come out. They take you by one arm and carry you to the edge of the floating platform, where they toss you off and out into space.

As you're falling, you wonder whether they think you can fly. "Not that it matters much," you say to a passing hawk.

The End

You find an exit at the far side of the demolished laboratory and locate it on the diagram. You follow a dark corridor. The light gets better as you come to a wall at the end.

Now you have to go either left or right. You look carefully at the diagram and follow the testing passageways each way with your finger. The route to the right may come to a dead end, or the symbol on the diagram may indicate a stairway going up or down. The route on the left leads to a room that could be Dr. Nekai's new laboratory. it's hard to be sure.

If you go to the left, turn to page 116.

If you go to the right, turn to page 82.

110

You take the hole on the left. Again you keep going through a series of chambers. Many of them lead to more than one other chamber. You have to choose again and again which way to go. By the time you realize you made the wrong choice, it's too late. You're hopelessly lost. There's no way of finding your way back. You're trapped in an endless maze.

The End

At the mention of the hyskos, the professor frowns. "The hyskos are our enemies, but first things first. We must stop the dragons before tackling our age-old problem of the hyskos regarding us only as food."

"I'll take the bottle," you say. "They understand that I want to stop the dragons."

"You are our only hope," Dr. Nekai says. He reaches into a cabinet and pulls out a bottle considerably larger than the ones he'd made before. "Do you think you can carry this? It's not as heavy as it looks."

You grab hold of the bottle. It's actually *heavier* than it looks, even in the light gravity of Tambor, but you don't intend to let that stop you. You thank Dr. Nekai and say good-bye, then struggle back to the surface with the bottle.

Turn to page 75.

Below you is a dragon, flying less than a hundred feet above the ground. It's twisting and turning and breathing fire downward, though it doesn't seem to be concerned about what's happening above it. Two hyskos land on its back and jab futilely with their spears.

You watch the dragon carefully. There's something almost mechanical about the creature. It looks like a dragon, but you wonder if these enemies of Tambor are actually artificial.

You catch up with the dragon and land on its back at midpoint. If the dragon isn't real, it should have two weak spots: its mouth, where it takes in air, and its sensors, most likely located in the bulge between its eyes.

If you attack the air intake, turn to page 86.

If you attack the sensors, turn to page 57.

When you come to, you're at the center of a curved surface. You're surrounded by large, bird-like humanoids, all wearing elaborate harnesses. Huge artificial wings are attached to them.

You sit up the best you can and look around. You're not sure exactly where you are, but you seem to be on top of a large balloon of some sort. To one side, you can see the desolate landscape of Tambor far below.

"What is this? What do you want with me?" you ask.

The creatures surrounding you grunt in response and look at each other with puzzled expressions.

Turn to page 97.

The boat was built for Derns, and because of its small size, it's awkward to row. Gradually you're able to move the craft. Slowly the opposite shore becomes clearer. You can make out little houses shaped like beehives. You see scores of Derns. They wave and gesture for you to come ashore. They look friendly enough, and you run toward them.

They *are* friendly, particularly after you tell them that Keesa sent you. They give you food and drink and soft bedding on which to sleep.

You stay with the Derns for many months, but Keesa never returns, and later you hear that he was killed by the dragons. The Derns tell you that someday the dragons will be defeated or die out. Then you'll be able to live once more on the surface, and perhaps even return to Earth. In the meantime, you hope desperately that they know what they're talking about!

The End

116

You go to the left and follow the twisting maze to a brightly lit room. Inside, Dr. Nekai is hunched over a workbench.

He looks up as you approach. "Ah! There you are again. Did you have any luck with the dragons? Never mind. I can see by your face that you didn't. I had to retreat down here. I had a particularly successful test of my acoustic bottles. I attracted lots of dragons. They landed so hard on the ground above my lab that they knocked down half the ceiling!"

"I'm glad you're safe," you say.

"And I'm glad you found me," Dr. Nekai replies, leaping up from his stool. "I've perfected my bottle! This one has a much wider range—it may cover the entire planet. That is, if I can figure out how to get it high enough in the sky."

"I think I could arrange that," you say.

"You can? How?" asks the scientist.

"The hyskos can—" you start.

Turn to page 111.

How sweet it is, when you come to, to see the friendly faces of Earthlings, helping you out of your battered spaceship. Good old Earth, you think. It's still the best planet in the galaxy.

The End

ABOUT THE AUTHOR

Richard Brightfield is a graduate of Johns Hopkins University, where he studied biology, psychology, and archaeology. For many years he worked as a graphic designer at Columbia University. He has written *The Deadly Shadow, Secret of the Pyramids, The Curse of Batterslea Hall, The Phantom Submarine, The Dragons' Den, The Secret Treasure of Tibet,* and *Invaders of the Planet Earth* in the Choose Your Own Adventure series and has coauthored more than a dozen game books with his wife, Glory. The Brightfields and their daughter, Savitri, live in Gardiner, New York.

ABOUT THE ILLUSTRATOR

Judith Mitchell was born and raised in New York City. She earned a Bachelor of Fine Arts degree from Chatham College and has also studied art at the Columbia University School of Arts and at the School of Visual Arts in New York City. Ms. Mitchell is the illustrator of *Outlaws of Sherwood Forest, Enchanted Kingdom, Mystery of the Secret Room, Seaside Mystery,* and *Space Vampire* in Bantam's Choose Your Own Adventure series. When the artist isn't working, she enjoys music, animals, cooking, collecting antiques, and travel. Judith Mitchell and her husband, Jack Murray, live in New York City.